Published by Greenleaf Book Group Press
Austin, Texas
www.gbgpress.com

Distributed by Greenleaf Book Group

For ordering information or special discounts for bulk purchases, please contact Greenleaf Book Group at PO Box 91869, Austin, TX 78709, 512.891.6100.

Design and composition by Greenleaf Book Group
Cover design by Greenleaf Book Group
Illustrations by David Miles

Publisher's Cataloging-in-Publication data is available.

Print ISBN: 978-1-62634-710-6
eBook ISBN: 978-1-62634-711-3

Part of the Tree Neutral® program, which offsets the number of trees consumed in the production and printing of this book by taking proactive steps, such as planting trees in direct proportion to the number of trees used: www.treeneutral.com

Manufactured through Asia Pacific Offset on acid-free paper
Manufactured in China, on January 2020
Batch No. Q19120050

20 21 22 23 24 25   10 9 8 7 6 5 4 3 2 1

First Edition

Thoughtful Honest Intelligent Necessary Kind

The Live Big Series—Book 3

THINK
BIG

A Mythological Fable About Animals Who
Discover How to Live Their Best Lives

KAT KRONENBERG

illustrated by David Miles

GREENLEAF
BOOK GROUP PRESS

Contained within these books is the wondrous fact that star dust lives above us, around us, and **within us all**. Watch the animals discover a third secret that lights the stars within their hearts. Try their secret and celebrate your best life together too, no matter the hardship!

In the wilds of East Africa,
thousands of years have passed since the savanna began. The animals continued to roam the land looking for food with this moody Baboon telling them what to do, when suddenly fear struck the land . . .

It began one rainy day with Giraffe starving, trying to eat some leaves while mumbling, "I can't reach. I'll never eat."

Nosy Baboon heard and couldn't help but sneer, "Wa-Hu-Wa-Hu-Think like that; you'll go hungry."

"Oh no," Giraffe groaned.
So he tried to climb.

He jumped.

He even piggybacked on Kudu.

But he lost his footing when curious Kudu moved to see the busy, buzzing Bee. Suddenly . . .

KAPOW! BOOM! WHACK!

The sky screamed. Lightning struck a tree! "FIRE!" Giraffe screeched, hitting the ground in pain.

"RUN!"

Baboon shrieked as the tree split in two.

"I can't!" Giraffe cried. "I hurt my knee! HELP ME UP, KUDU! PLEASE!"

But Kudu had run after Baboon.

Baboon noticed and couldn't help but sneer, "Wa-Hu-Wa-Hu-Kudu, didn't you hear Giraffe cry out to you?"

"Yeah but," Kudu panicked.
"I'm scared. What **do** I **do**?"

Kudu took a thoughtful
breath, and then turned and
ran back to help his friend.
Kudu jumped and sprang
over hot, fiery flames to bump
Giraffe to his feet.

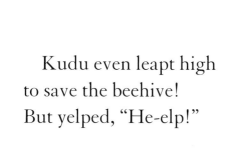

Kudu even leapt high
to save the beehive!
But yelped, "He-elp!"

Kudu's tail was on fire!
Beyond scared, Kudu got
out of there, racing with
Giraffe to the Baobab Tree.

Kudu found a puddle.
Plop! PSHhhe! Then
he collapsed with fear,
muttering, "Life's too
scary for me. I quit."

Baboon heard and
couldn't help but sneer,
"Wa-Hu-Wa-Hu-Giraffe,
do something. Kudu just
saved you!"

13

"Yeah but," Giraffe grunted. "I don't know. What do I do?"

Giraffe took a thoughtful breath, and feeling his brain and heart connect, he smiled big with a brilliant idea.

With his neck
growing longer,
Giraffe strived to
reach the leaves again
and again, as he
stomped and clapped,
"I believe in me!
I AM extraordinary!
I can—"

WHOOSH! WHAM! I CAN GO FOR EXTRAORDINARY!

YES! Giraffe* did it! Using his extraordinary, long neck, he easily grabbed some leaves. He gave them to Kudu and said, "This fresh food can help you feel better! And THANK YOU! Your bravery taught me to *stick my neck out and go for it*—and what a view!"

But Kudu didn't move. He just lay there, shaking in fear.

Of course, Bossy Baboon couldn't help but sneer, "Wa-Hu-Wa-Hu-Do something, Bee! Kudu saved you too!"

*Giraffes are the tallest land mammal, which allows them to find their food in trees and grab it with the their long, bluish tongue.

"Yeah but," buzzed Bee. "What **do I do**?"

Bee took a thoughtful breath, and feeling her brain
and heart connect, she smiled big with a great idea.

Busy Bee flew toward the fragrant flowers to put her plan to work, clapping on the way.

"I believe in me! I AM great! I AM thoughtful! I can—"

WHOOSH! WHAM!
I CAN BE GRATEFUL!

YES! Busy Bee* was so grateful to be alive and thankful Kudu saved her hive that she started dancing and singing, "My life is full of aBunDANCE!" Her dance moves were brilliant! *They made an actual map that her Bee Community could follow to find flowers and collect enough nectar to make Kudu a new comfort food.*

*Bees use their "bun-dance moves" called the *waggle* and the *round* to show their community where to find flowers. They collect nectar from these flowers to make their honey.

TO DO GOOD!

They proudly gave it to Kudu and said, "THANK YOU! Hopefully, our new sweet-honey treat can comfort you from the scary challenge you faced to save us!"

But Kudu didn't even move to eat the yummy-smelling treat.

Right then, Brilliant Baboon swung down and howled. "YES! Kudu, I know what to do. There's another powerful secret—SHHH!—we can all use." Baboon put a hand on Kudu's shoulder and said, "Don't quit! THINK BIG! Consider who you want to be; know that we are all born extraordinary. Celebrate your possibility and ideas. Shout "I AM—"

What do you do?

With a do-do dilemma?

"Yeah, but I can't," interrupted Kudu, quaking with fear. "The fiery flames are right there!"

Big-eared Elephant came to the rescue, trumpeting to Kudu, "Baboon's right! The secret— SHHH—works!

It's how I put these dangerous flames out! I AM strong! I AM fearless!"

"YES," buzzed Busy Bee!
"The secret helps me *bee*
all I can *bee*, and I AM
unbelievably amazing!"

"YES!" Bush Baby added,
"It reminds me I AM loved and
cherished, so I can hang through
any crisis! You can too!"

"Yeah but I quit,"
barked Kudu.
"So leave me alone."

After a thoughtful
breath, Baboon got
Bee, and together they
wrote Kudu a song.
Sing along:

DO Good

*Twinkle, twinkle, know you are
Brave and kind so light your stars
Smile "I can" and dare Believe
Thinking Big we all succeed
Twinkle, twinkle, hearts of stars
Guiding us we all go far

*Baboon and Bee's song is sung to the tune "Twinkle, Twinkle, Little Star." Sing along!

As they sang, the wind changed direction.

WHOOSH! SNAP! POP!

Fire surrounded them, as Baboon nervously sneered,
"Wa-Hu-Wa-Hu-What **do** we **do**? Without help we can't survive!"

Baobab Tree took a thoughtful breath, and feeling its brain and heart connect, it smiled big with a grand idea.

With the help of big-eared Elephant, Baobab Tree began to hollow out its trunk as it swayed in the breeze, clapping, "I believe in good! I believe in all of you! I AM powerful too! I can—"

WHOOSH !
WHAM !
I CAN GIVE TO LIVE
AND LIVE
TO GIVE!

YES! Grateful Baboon and Kudu knew they could be safe from the flames in Baobab's new, awesome, hollowed-out Clubhouse.* Encouraged, Kudu hopped to his feet, ate the leaves, and grabbed Bee's sweet-honey treat, but . . .

Wait!

*Baobab Trees, nicknamed The Tree of Life, help communities thrive with all they have to give from food to safety to medicine. One community even used the trunk of a thousand-year-old tree as a pub that fit 60 people.

Kudu saw terror in Bush Baby's eyes. She was falling from the tree, wailing, "HELP ME AND MY BABY!"

"Oh no!" Kudu panicked. "What **do I do**?"

Kudu took a thoughtful breath, and feeling his brain and
heart connect, he smiled big with the perfect idea.

With his horns continuing to grow, Kudu stomped and clapped,
"I'll never quit! I AM brave! I AM kind! I can—"

WHOOSH! WHAM!
I CAN BE THE
BEST ME!

YES! Kudu* bravely saved Bush Baby and her baby from the flames! Kudu laid them safely in Baobab's Clubhouse with Bee's sweet-honey treat and celebrated with Baboon, saying, "There's no doubt we can get through anything together! So please try the SHHH—secret—too! No matter what happens, never quit! THINK BIG! Feel your head and heart connect with a big inside SMILE and BELIEVE!"

*As they mature, tradition says Kudus grow long, beautiful, twisting horns to represent the good choices they make when faced with hard, unexpected twists of fate.

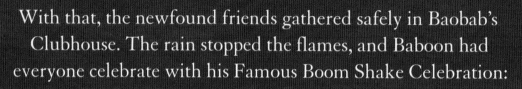

With that, the newfound friends gathered safely in Baobab's Clubhouse. The rain stopped the flames, and Baboon had everyone celebrate with his Famous Boom Shake Celebration:

"Wa-Whoo!
Shake your pompoms.
Smile big with grand ideas!
Live out your YES!
Knowing hearts of stars are lit!

NOTES FOR TWO-LEGGERS OF ALL AGES:

—SHHH—

Have fun learning more about these fascinating animals and tree on Kat's website. We can learn so much from their lives, and let's all try their—SHHH—secret, so no matter what hardship we face, we too can celebrate our best lives together.

Did you see what happened to the animals when they tried the secret? Their hidden hearts of stars got lit up! Baboon's Baby Girl calls this experience catching CATCH-M!

CATCH-M is the name of our miraculous inside SMILE that invites the wondrous star dust within us to *WHOOSH* through our bodies & *WHAM* connect with the star dust in our hearts, igniting the BELIEF we need to THINK BIG & solve problems together.

Baboon's Baby came up with this catchy nickname as our reminder. She also has some fun things you can do alone, with family, friends, or in a classroom to learn to THINK BIG so that we can live our best lives & "catch CATCH-M" too-gather!

(Share your fun with our LIVE BIG COMMUNITY using #LiveBig or #CatchM on social media.)

"We are made of star-stuff. There are pieces of star within us all . . . Every one of us is, in the cosmic perspective, precious."—Carl Sagan

1. Create Your Own CATCH-M

"S. M. I. L. E.—**S**ee **M**iracles **I**n **L**ife **E**very Day!"—Kennedy Joy Stokes

Go back through the book. Find scenes where CATCH-M is shining in each animal's heart. Then take time to draw your inside smile—a close-your-eyes-take-a-deep-breath, big SMILE that comes all the way up from your belly & connects your heart to your head!

Use your smile to remember you can take a thoughtful breath when faced with hard times and choose to do good with your ideas!

Take your smile on a **CATCH-M ADVENTURE**: on a trip, to school, or wherever you go. On your adventure, build a LIVE BIG Club, as you remind others to celebrate their smiles, too! Take pictures and journal as you go. Then find as many ways in a day to catch CATCH-M by smiling big with grand ideas and problem solving together!

"The most important question you can ask yourself is,
Is the universe a friendly place?"
—Albert Einstein

2. Be extraordinary—stick your neck out

Be like Giraffe! Learn what you need and enjoy. Know your Goals. Write them down or use the "Go Big Goal Sandwich Download" on Kat's website!

Make a plan to go for your **G**oals, to go for extraordinary! Take chances. Stick your neck out, and on your quest to guarantee success, find three ways to **G**ive & be **G**rateful every day. With the biggest heart of any land mammal, Giraffe realized these three Gs—**G**oals, **G**ifts, and **G**ratitude—can turn any life event into an extraordinary adventure where dreams do come true!

3. Be great-full—play the "A-BUN-Dance Game"

Be like Queen Bee! Be grateful! Develop an attitude of gratitude—Every day, start with three thank yous. Then, when things get hard, scary, lonely, or confusing, play the "A-BUN-Dance Game." Put on a tutu, crown, headband, or anything grand. Pull out your pompoms or drums.

Celebrate that you are born great! The only you who will ever be. Believe in your possibility & ideas! THINK BIG! Shout "I AM" statements. "I AM *great*! I AM *thoughtful*!"

Then break into Bee's Bun-Dance by shaking your bum & singing, "MY LIFE IS FULL OF A-BUN-DANCE!"

Abundance is defined as a state of prosperity!

Have fun! Shake your **buns**! Pound your drum! Believe it to be true & see the great ideas that come up for you!

4. Be giving—Celebrate you and your community with a *family tree*

Be like Baobab Tree! Learn to be generous—share food, water, safety, shelter, medicine, & more with those around you—see how much it blesses you. Baobab Trees can live thousands of years as they celebrate, share, & enjoy their community!

Celebrate you & your community too by drawing your Family Tree:

★ On each branch of your tree, write the names of your family: those who are related, and those whom you have chosen.

★ As you write their names, learn about each family member.

★ On the fruit of the tree, write the name of friends, people, & animals you believe in & depend on. Consider why.

★ Finally, on the trunk of your tree, write who you are, your goals, gifts, & passions that only you can share with the world.

Feel your roots go deep into the earth. From this safe, sturdy, & powerful place, plan three ways every day to give, to live a long, fruitful, & fantastic life like Baobab Tree!

5. Be the best you—celebrate with the "No Bad But Game"

Be like Kudu! Learn the different ways you can respond to tough times & unexpected twists in fate.
    Start by noticing when, where, or why the word "but" might come out of your mouth.

If "but" is a possibility, slow down, take time to understand your moods, what you do, or how you think:

★ Are you in **flight** mode— ready to run away & avoid your problems?

★ Are you **frozen with fear**—so scared you can hardly function & want to quit?

★ Are you in **fight mode**—ready to argue & unable to listen?

Go to Kat's website to learn more about the "No Bad But Game."
    YES—to win the game: First, remember you can never say the oxymoron: "Yeah, but___." For example: "Yeah, but I can't;" "Yeah, but I am scared;" or "Yeah, but I don't know what to do." Second, every day celebrate that you are great with the 3 Gs: 3 Goals, Gifts, and Gratitude.

6. Termite tricks to encourage—plus Dung Beetle's trick & more

A. Dung Beetle's DO-DO DILEMMA—WHAT DO YOU DO?
Be like Dung Beetle who learned an important lesson in the book, *Love Big*. What **DO** you **DO** in a bad, hard, or scary situation? Or in Dung Beetle's case with an actual pile of doo-doo? Go back through the book to see what they say. Notice Queen Bee reinforces their message on her trail map to the flowers. Also, enjoy Dung Beetle's "DO-DO Game" on Kat's website.

(Dung Beetle's question is on page 26: Their answer is on page 30 : "Do good!" Queen Bee's message is on pages 24-25: "We are all born to do good!")

B. Headband Fun for "The A-BUN-Dance Game"
Notice Baboon's, Baby Baboon's, Giraffe's, & Elephant's headbands in the book.

(Baboon's says, "I AM"; Baby Baboon's says, "You can tutu"; Giraffe's says, "Party"; and Elephant's says, "Live Big.")

C. Termite Tricks
Solve The Termite Tricks & use them to help you write ones that encourage others too:

★ Page 16: Termites have the letters I K-N on their back to remind us that…?

★ Page 22: Termites have the letters B GR8 on their back to remind us that…?

★ Page 26: Termites have the letters B-L-V on their back to remind us that…?

★ Page 30: Termites have the letters U-R on their back to remind us that…?

★ Page 34: Termites have the letters B G-N-R-S on their back to remind us that…?

★ Page 40: Termites have the letters B U-R B-S-T on their back to remind us to…?

★ Page 36 & 42: Termites arranged the letters & number C L 8 U for fun to remind us to…?

★ Page 48: Termites have the letters T-H-I-N-K on their back while holding signs to remind us what to do when life gets hard.

(Answers: P. 16—I can; P. 22—Be great; P. 26—Believe; P. 30—You are; P. 34—Be generous; P. 40—Be your best; P. 36 & 42—Celebrate you and smile; P. 48—Thoughtful, Honest, Intelligent, Necessary, & Kind.)

To THINK BIG, find more fun, see Go Big Goal Sandwiches, play the "A-BUN-Dance Game" or the "No Bad But Game," visit Kat's website: www.katkronenberg.com.

Now it's your turn! Make a pledge! When you are faced with a hard situation or a tough choice, try the— SHHH—secret, too! There is no telling what great ideas will come up for you!

Close your eyes.
Take three THINK BIG breaths as your head and heart connect.
Be Grateful!
Be Giving!
Be the best you & Go for extraordinary!
SMILE big in All that is!
Clap, "I BELIVE IN ME! I BELIEVE IN YOU! I BELIEVE IN GOOD!
I AM . . ."
And—Whoosh! Wham!—
I can . . .

(The proceeds from *Think Big* will go to support other Two-Leggers' dreams as we celebrate the magic and marvel of WE:

www.we.org, www.grameenamerica.org, & www.donorschoose.org.)

"A smile is a U-SHAPED BRIDGE that can connect us to everything—**our head to our hearts,** our lives to one another, & our dreams to the power of something GREATER! So, let's all catch CATCH-M too, celebrate that we can get through anything together, & watch our lives shine!"
—Kat Kronenberg